10⁹⁵⁻

GRANDPA'S WITCHED-UP CHRISTMAS

Grandpa's Witched-up Christmas

Story and pictures by
JAMES FLORA

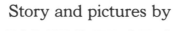

A MARGARET K. McELDERRY BOOK

ATHENEUM 1982

NEW YORK

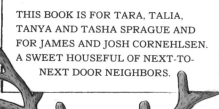

THIS BOOK IS FOR TARA, TALIA,
TANYA AND TASHA SPRAGUE AND
FOR JAMES AND JOSH CORNEHLSEN.
A SWEET HOUSEFUL OF NEXT-TO-
NEXT DOOR NEIGHBORS.

Library of Congress catalog card number 81-12843
ISBN 0-689-50232-X
Copyright © 1982 by James Flora
Published simultaneously in Canada
by McClelland & Stewart, Ltd.
Manufactured in the United States of America
Printed by Connecticut Printers, Inc., Hartford
Bound by Halliday Lithograph Company, Inc.
West Hanover, Massachusetts
First Edition

ast Christmas I was helping Grandpa decorate his tree. While we were stringing the tinsel, he said, "Did you ever miss a Christmas?"

"No," I said. "I never did and I hope I never do. Did you ever miss one?"

"Almost. When I was eight years old. It was touch and go, I'll tell you. I get the shivers even now when I think of it."

"Tell me about it," I begged.

"If I told you, it might scare Christmas right out of you."

"No it won't, Grandpa. You know I like your scary stories. Please tell me."

"Very well. I don't mind if I do," Grandpa said. "And I will if you will just turn the page."

He sat down. I climbed on his lap and turned the page.

"It was the afternoon before Christmas. I was skating on the pond with some friends when someone's mother called to us, 'It's getting late. You had best get home before Santa comes.'

"All of us took off our skates and hurried for home because everybody knows that if you aren't snug in your bed Santa won't leave any presents for you.

"I took a shortcut through the woods, though I knew it was the wrong thing to do."

"Why was it wrong?" I asked.

"Because there are only two paths through that forest and the place where they meet is called 'The Witches' Crossroad.' Lots of people have gone into that forest and some of them never

came out. I thought I could hurry through before it got dark but
that was my big mistake. When I reached the crossroad I saw a
witch coming down the path toward me.

"I turned and ran up the other path. I hadn't gone far when I
saw another witch floating down *that* path on her broom. I hurried back and, horror of horrors, there was a third witch walking
down *that* path.

"I was scared to death, so I climbed high up an old oak tree.
It wasn't much of a place to hide, since it was winter and there
were no leaves on the tree. At least it was better than being
caught by the witches.

"Those witches were a fearsome lot. They wore ragged black capes and carried greasy sacks slung over their shoulders. I knew what was in those sacks—children's finger bones, dead cats, dried bats and hop toads. Those are the sorts of things witches use to make their magic.

"The first witch was fat and dumpy, with sharp teeth and hair like an unmowed lawn. The second witch was so old and shrunken she looked like a skeleton. She didn't have any feet. That's why she rode a broom. The third witch was tall and warty. She wore a real pointed witch's hat. Her eyes would make a polecat shiver.

"They came together just under my tree and hugged each other, chattering like a tree full of crows.

" 'Peggoty dear, it's good to see you again after all of these years,' said the first witch.

" 'It has been a long time,' cackled the second witch. 'Seems to me it was thirty years ago at the big baby roast.'

" 'No it wasn't, darling,' said the third witch. 'It was forty years ago. The time we burned all of the barns in Indiana.'

" 'No matter when it was, it's nice to be together again. I'll bet you two have learned plenty of new tricks,' the first witch said.

" 'Oh my, indeed we have,' the other two screeched.

" 'So have I,' cackled the first witch. 'Let me show you a nice nasty one. See that boy who thinks he's hiding in the tree? Watch this.'

"She pointed her finger at me and squealed, 'SHAZAM!'

"All at once I felt my body changing," Grandpa said. "It didn't hurt. It just felt funny. I knew I wasn't a boy any more. I was something else. I opened my mouth to scream but I could only hiss. A long forked tongue flicked out of my mouth. I turned my head to see my body.

"I WAS A SNAKE! A big, thick, green snake.

"Down below the witches howled with glee.

" 'Very nice, dear,' shrieked the second witch. 'But I can do better than that. Watch this.'

"She pointed her finger to where I was slithering along the tree limb.

" 'OLLY-POGGLE!' she cried.

"Once again I could feel my body change. I looked around. I had claws and tail feathers. I lifted my wings and flew into the air. I was a big bird. A turkey buzzard.

" 'Clever. Very clever. An adorable trick,' Peggoty cried. 'Now watch this one.'

"I was flying higher and higher," Grandpa said. "I really liked being a bird. Now I would be able to fly away from those witches. I was just soaring over the treetops when Peggoty, the third witch, pointed her long, dirty finger at me and screamed, 'TA-POOTY!'

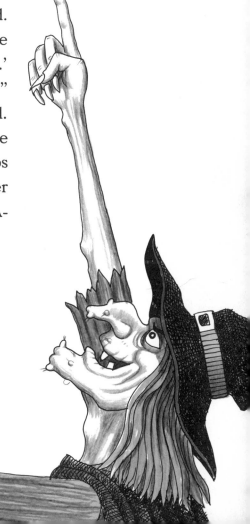

"In a flash my body had changed again and I began to fall. I didn't have time to see what I had become. I fell plop into a chinaberry bush. It knocked the wind out of me.

"The witches thought it was so funny they rolled around on the ground screaming with laughter.

" 'A darling trick, Peggoty. Now we can have pork chops for dinner.' They squealed and giggled.

"I began to run as soon as I caught my wind. I looked down. I had hooves instead of feet. Was I a horse or a pony? I looked over my shoulder to see if I had a horse's tail. I didn't. I had a curly tail.

"I WAS A PIG!

"I squealed with fright and ran off through the woods. The witches didn't bother to chase me. They were too busy laughing and showing off their mean tricks. Soon I was safely far away, but I was still a pig. What should I do now?

"I ran for home. I hoped my mother or dad could help me. At least I wanted to be snug in bed before Santa came.

"I was out of breath when I got to my house. I tried to turn the doorknob but my little piggy feet couldn't do it. My mother heard me scratching and opened the door. I rushed in squealing and tried to hug her.

"She screamed with fright and pushed me away. She ran into the kitchen and slammed the door in my face.

" 'SAM! SAM! HELP!' she called to my father. 'There's a wild pig in the living room.'

" 'No, Mama,' I shouted. 'It's not a wild pig. It's me. Your little boy.'

"But of course she couldn't understand me because I could only squeal like a pig.

"The door opened and my daddy came into the room with a coal shovel in his hands. I ran to him crying, 'It's me, Daddy. Your son. Your own little boy.'

"But all that came from my mouth was, 'OINK-OINK-OINK!'

"My daddy swatted me with the shovel. Ouch, it hurt. I ran around the room squealing. I tried to run upstairs to my bed. Daddy grabbed my legs and pulled me down again. He dragged me to the door, pushed me out and slammed it behind me.

"Oh, it was terrible, being out there in the cold night on Christmas Eve. Locked out by my own mother and dad. I wept. Through the window I could see the warm fire in the fireplace and our Christmas tree with its blinking lights. I whimpered and moaned. Tears rolled down my piggy snout. Oh how I wanted to be in there safe and snug.

"Sadly I turned away. It was bitter cold and I had to walk to keep warm. I walked and walked and thought and thought. Suddenly it came to me. There was only one thing to do. Find Peggoty, the witch, and beg her to make me into a boy once again.

"I stumbled back into that dark, dark forest. I hoped all of the hungry wolves were fast asleep in their dens. An owl hooted and I almost jumped out of my skin. Even pigs get scared.

" 'Sorry about that,' said the owl. 'But I have to hoot once in a while to keep from freezing.'

" 'That's all right,' I said. 'I have to walk for the same reason. Can you tell me where Peggoty the witch lives? I was a boy this afternoon and she made me into a pig. If I can find her I'm going to ask her to turn me into a boy once again so I can go home and be snug in my bed before Santa comes.'

" 'I know just how you feel,' said the owl. 'Yesterday I was a little girl named Ida May until Peggoty turned me into a hootie owl. Now my mother and dad won't let me into the house. My mother is afraid of owls.'

" 'Let's find the witch together. Since it is Christmas Eve, even a witch may feel enough Christmas spirit to give us back our bodies.'

" 'I wouldn't count on that. Witches are too mean and nasty. They hate Christmas,' said Ida May. 'But we can try. Follow me and I'll take you to her house. It's deep in the forest. You would never find it by yourself.'

"She flitted from tree to tree while I stumbled along below her. The forest was so thick and thorny that I was covered with scratches by the time we reached Peggoty's house.

"What a house it was. You knew right away that a witch had to live there. It was patched together with old boards and had a roof like a witch's hat. Even the chimney had a witch hat on it. Big, fierce-looking crows sat on the roof glaring at us with fiery eyes. A pile of dead rats and mangy cats lay beside the rain spout and the weather vane was made with a skull and cross-bones.

"It was so scary that Ida May perched on my head and shivered. Before I could knock, the crows set up such a racket the the door flew open. There stood the witch.

" 'Good evening, Miss Peggoty,' I said. 'Since it is Christmas Eve, we thought you might turn us back into the boy and girl we once were. Then we could go home and be snug in bed before Santa comes.'

"Peggoty smiled a horrible smile. She only had two teeth in her mouth.

" 'Come in, my darlings, my dears,' she crooned. 'Do come in and we'll have a nice chat about it.'

"Inside, the house was just as ghastly as the outside. There were a few rickety chairs and a filthy table. The floor was thick with old bones and chicken feathers. Pictures of ghouls and demons hung on the wall, and those evil crows flew in with us and perched everywhere.

"Peggoty slammed the door shut.

" 'HEE-HEE-HEE!' she screeched. 'You are just in time for Christmas dinner. Indeed, my sweets, you shall be my Christmas dinner. I'll start with a tasty bowl of owl soup and follow that with a fine roast pig. I'll even put an apple in your mouth, darling.'

"I hid under the table while the witch tried to catch Ida May. She kicked at me and snatched at Ida. She tried to knock her down with a broom. But Ida May was very fluttery and managed to fly up the chimney. As she left she called out to me, 'I'll get help.'

"Peggoty screamed with rage.

" 'CATCH HER, CROWS. BRING HER BACK TO ME.'

"She unlatched a shutter and the crows swooped out. I wasn't afraid for Ida May. I knew that crows can't see well at night, but hootie owls can. I was afraid for *me*. Peggoty snatched my hind leg, dropped me into a huge pot of water and lit a fire under it.

" 'A little boiling will make you nice and tender before I put you to roast,' she cackled and stirred me about with a big wooden spoon.

"She sprinkled me with salt until my eyes were burning. She shook pepper on me until I snuffled and sneezed.

" 'Very nice,' she crooned. 'You are going to be a very tasty dish, my dear.'

"The water was getting so hot that I had to dance about to keep from burning my feet. I began to squeal with pain. If you

have never been boiled alive you can't know how much it hurts.
I was in despair. It was too late for Ida May to bring help now.
I might as well give up and be boiled.

"Suddenly the door smashed open and a loud voice roared,
'UNPOT THAT PIG, YOU FIEND. 'TIS CHRISTMAS EVE!'

" 'I WON'T. I WON'T. I WON'T,' the witch screamed.

" 'YOU WILL. YOU WILL. YOU WILL,' the big voice roared.

"My eyes were so full of salt I couldn't see who belonged to
that great voice. Finally I blinked them clear and looked.

"IT WAS SANTA CLAUS!

"With one hand he grabbed the witch by the neck and shook her. With the other hand he plucked me from the pot. Just in time, too. I was beginning to turn red.

" 'And now, you foul fiend,' Santa cried, 'practice your magic art and return these children to their former bodies.'

" *'I won't, I won't,'* choked the witch.

" *'You will. Else I'll squeeze some Christmas spirit into you.'*

"Santa squeezed harder and harder on her skinny neck. Peggoty's face turned red, then blue, then green. Her tongue popped out. She gasped, *'I have it. I have the Christmas spirit.'*

" 'I knew it would come to you. It comes to all of us at some time or other,' Santa said.

"Old Peggoty pointed a bony finger at us and said, 'TAPOOTY! TAPOOTY!'

"The words were barely out of her mouth when we began to glow and tingle. I looked at Ida May. She was growing fast. Her feathers and wings were gone and as I watched she turned into the prettiest little girl I had ever seen.

"I looked and saw that I was my old self once again," Grandpa said. "With the same brown coat and the same old scruffy shoes. I held Ida May's hand and thanked her for my rescue."

" 'When I flew up the chimney Santa's sleigh was just passing over,' Ida May said. 'I swooped up and hooted in Santa's ear. Wasn't he nice to come down and save us?'

" 'I love you, Santa Claus,' I said.

" 'I love you too,' Santa said. 'But now it is time to go. You should be home and snug in bed before I come, else you may not get any presents.'

" 'We'll never be able to get through the woods and climb into bed in time,' Ida May said. 'It is too far.'

" 'Oh yes you will, because I'm taking you with me,' Santa said, and he put us in his sleigh. Ida May sat in front with Santa and I sat in the back with all of the presents.

" 'UP! UP AND AWAY!' Santa shouted. 'On Donner! On Blitzen! Let's scramble. Time is wasting.'

"Those eight tiny reindeer soon had us soaring through the sky. It was grand riding with Santa. We all sang Christmas songs. Ida May had a comb in her school bag and she combed Santa's long white beard. Soon we could see lights below.

" 'There it is. There is my house,' I cried.

"The sleigh glided down to a soft landing on the roof.

" 'I'll go down the chimney first,' said Santa. 'Then you follow. Do as I do. Just lay your finger alongside your nose and let yourself go.'

"We did and when I came out of the fireplace Santa was saying to my mother and dad, 'Here is your Christmas boy. Safe and sound.'

"My mom and dad hugged me and fussed over me. 'This is Ida May,' I said. 'She was once a little hootie owl. Isn't she pretty? Santa is going to take her home.'

"Then I scampered upstairs and popped into my snug, warm bed with hopes that Santa would leave me some presents. He did too. Mighty fine ones they were," Grandpa said. "And that is the story of the Christmas I almost missed."

"Aw, Grandpa! Is that a true story or did you just make it up?"

"It's as true as true is," Grandpa said. "Just to show you how true it is I'll tell you this. When that sweet little Ida May grew up to be a woman, I married her. She is your grandmother. The very same grandmother who is sitting in the next room. You can ask her if this story isn't true."

I ran to the next room.

"Grandma, were you ever a little hootie owl named Ida May? Did you meet Grandpa deep in the forest when he was a pig? Did you go to the witch's house with him and ride home on Santa's sleigh? Did you?"

"Land's sake! Good heavens! My goodness, no. Never," Grandma said. "My name is Ida May, sure enough, but I never did any of the other things. I'll bet your grandfather has been telling you another of his crazy stories. Hasn't he?"

"Now I know that Grandpa made it up!" I said. "But it was a grand story. I liked it a lot. I think my grandpa is the nicest grandpa in the whole world."

"I'll drink to that," Grandma said. And she did.

She had rose petal tea.

I had buttermilk.

We both had cookies.

It was a grand Christmas.

C.1

E
F
Flora, James

Grandpa's witched-up
Christmas

D

DATE			
Fry			